PATOR DAN SAYS COLOR SOME SKULLS!

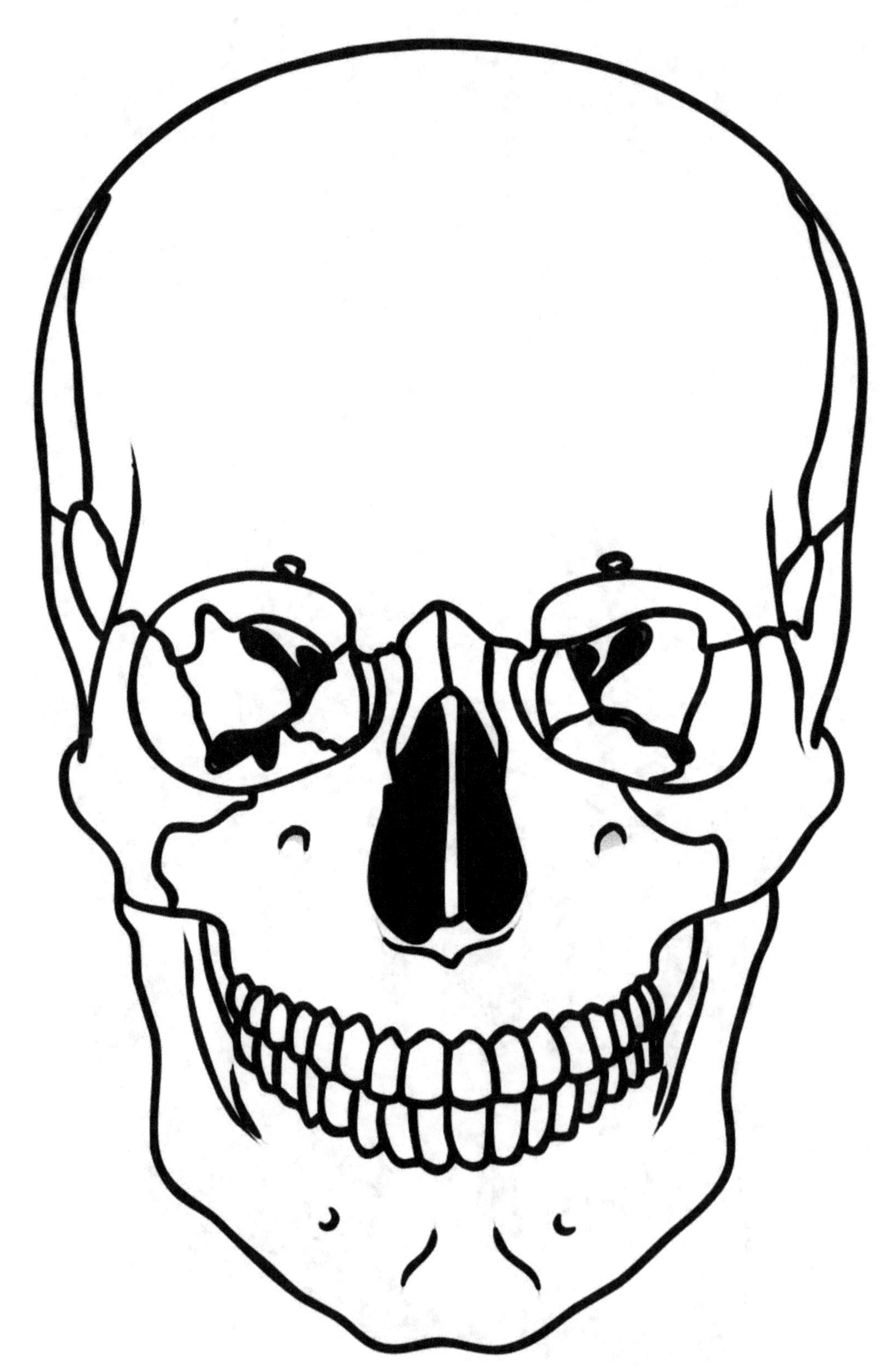

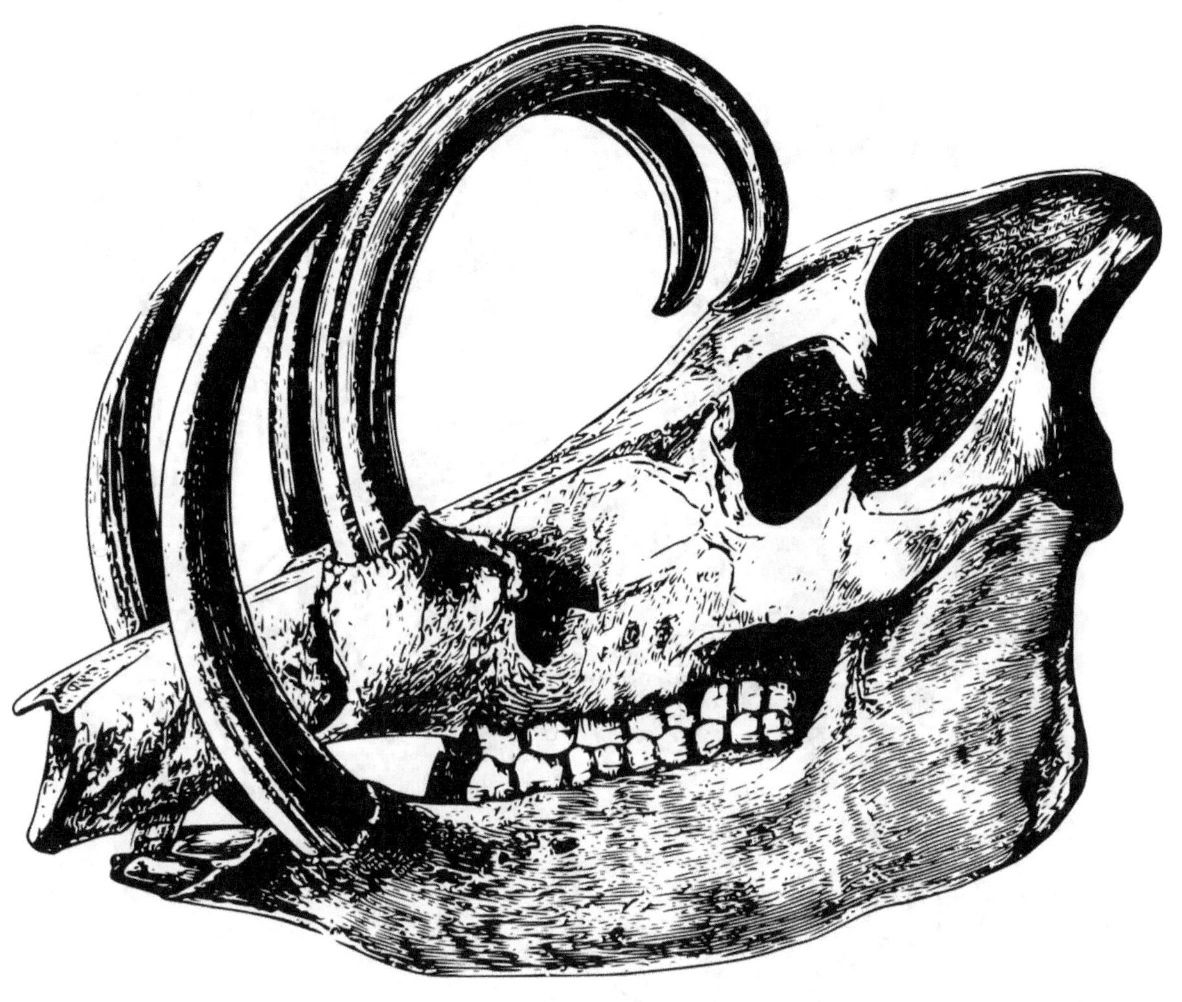

BOO!

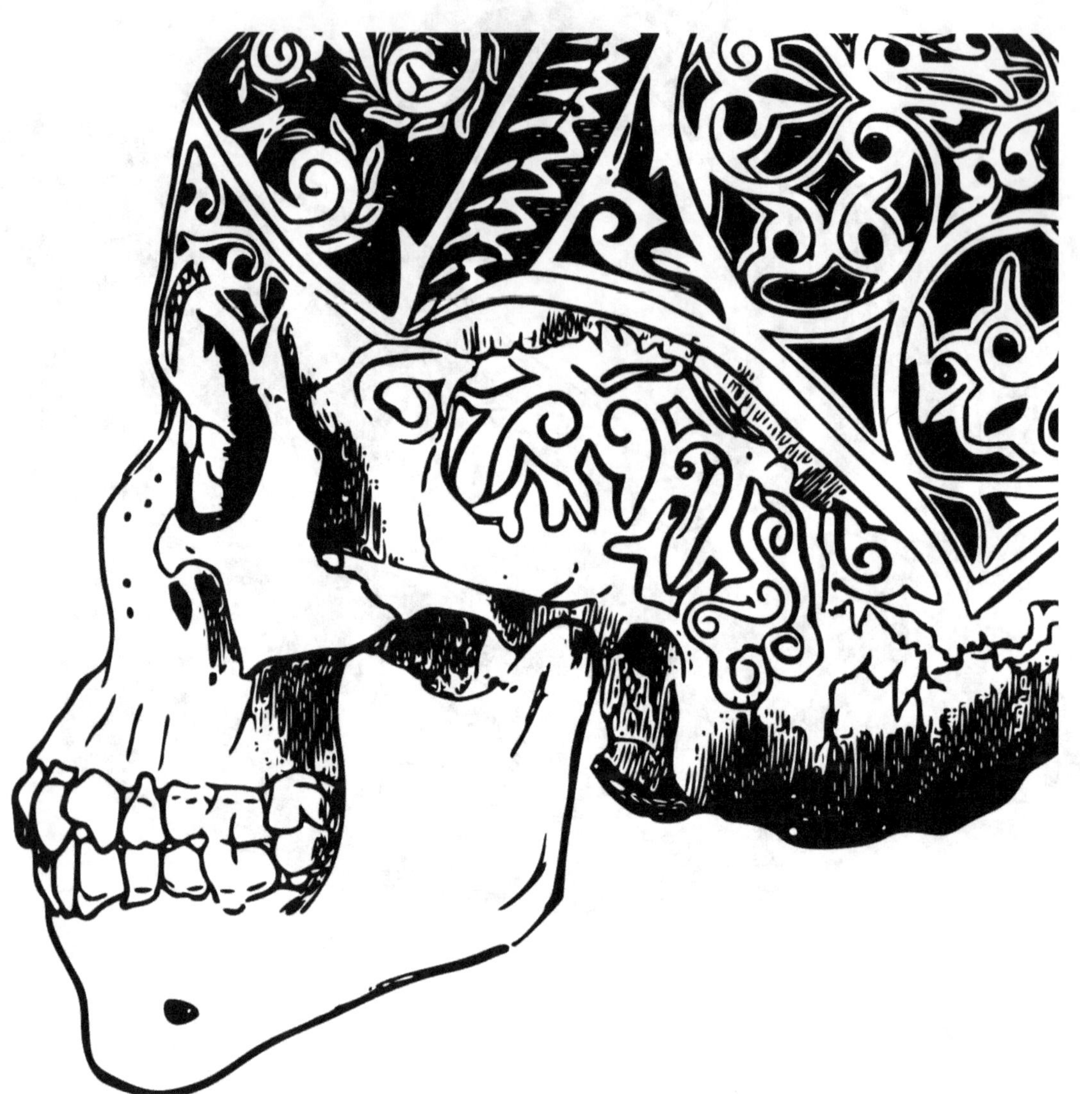

SCARY!

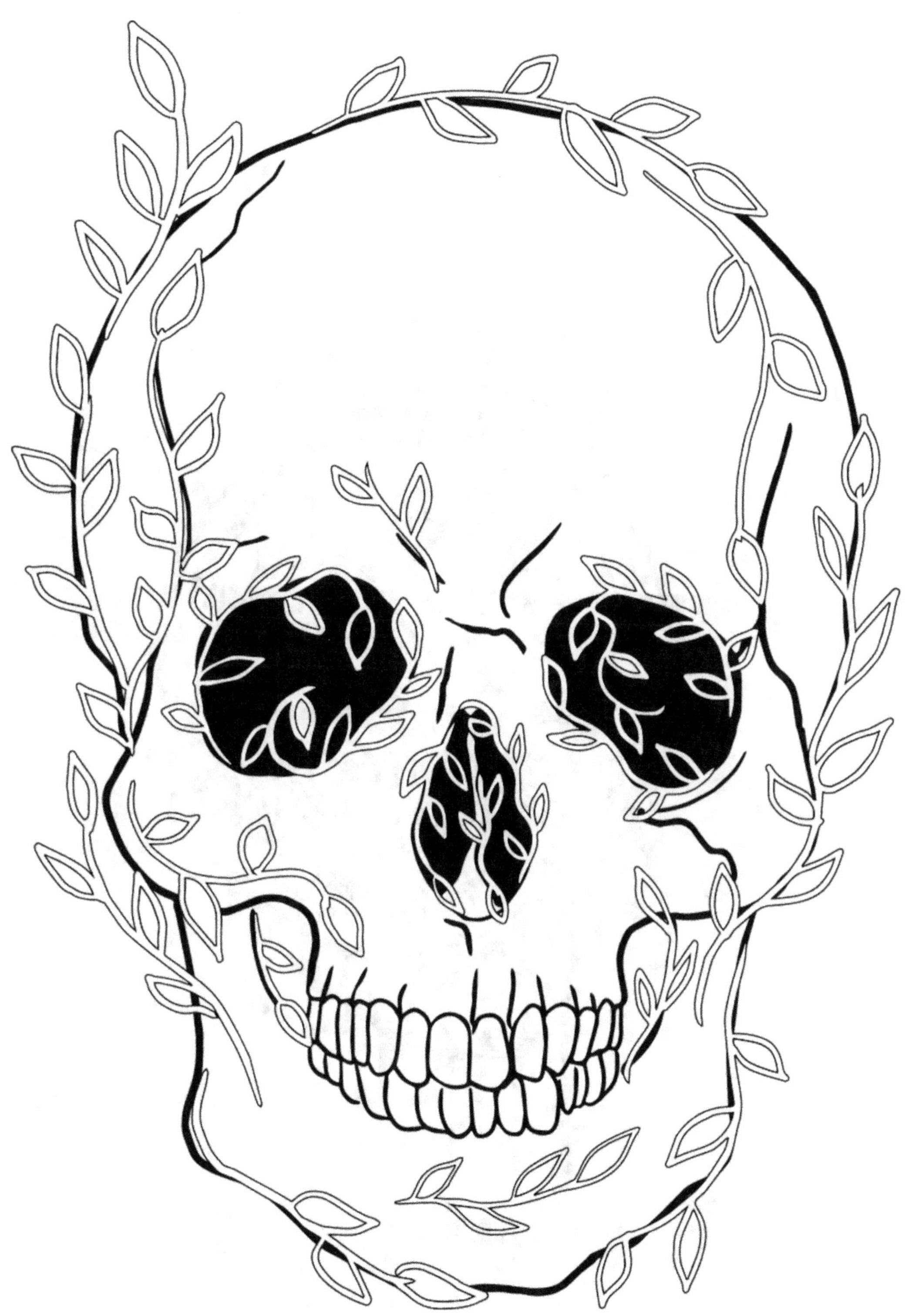

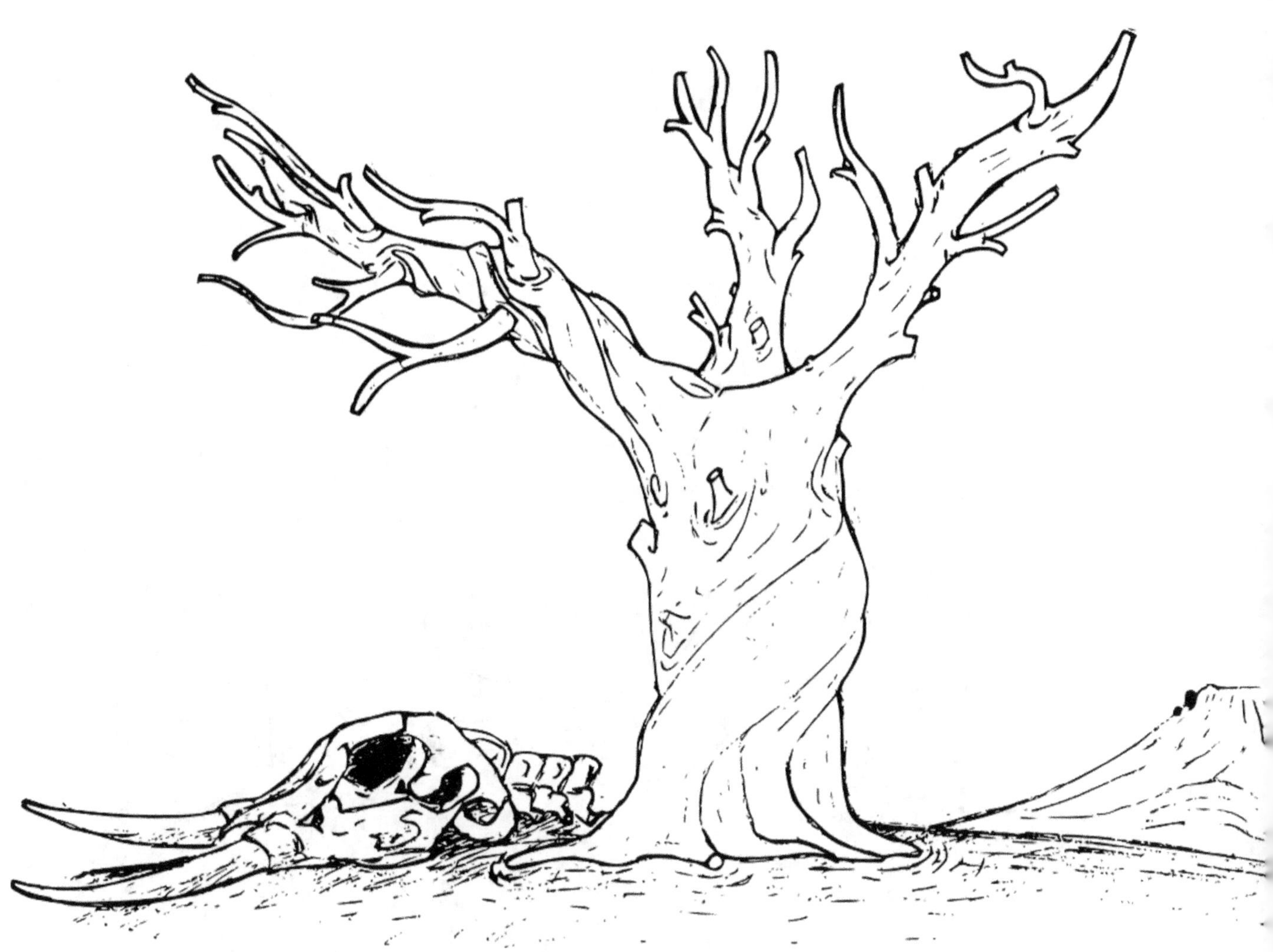

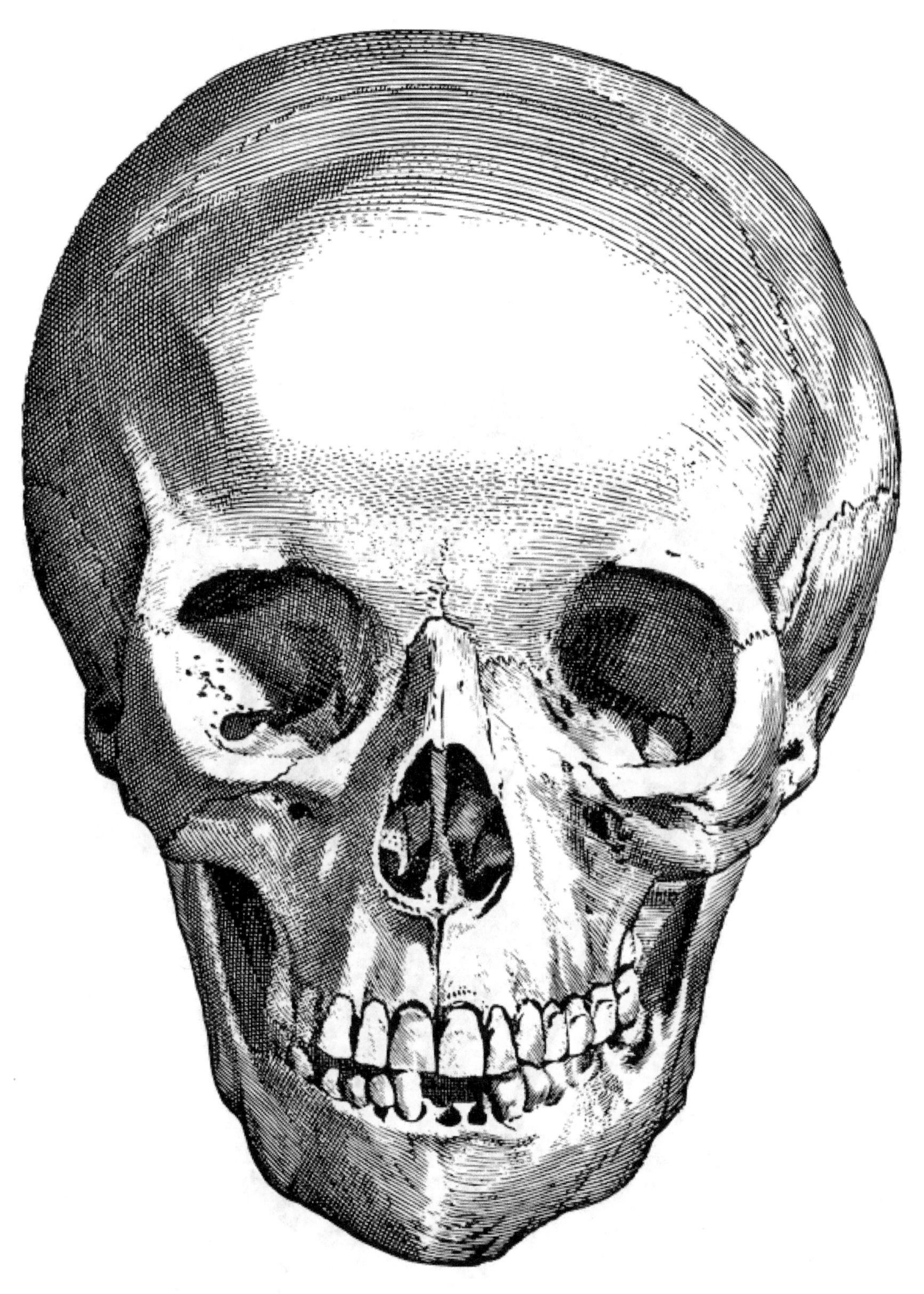

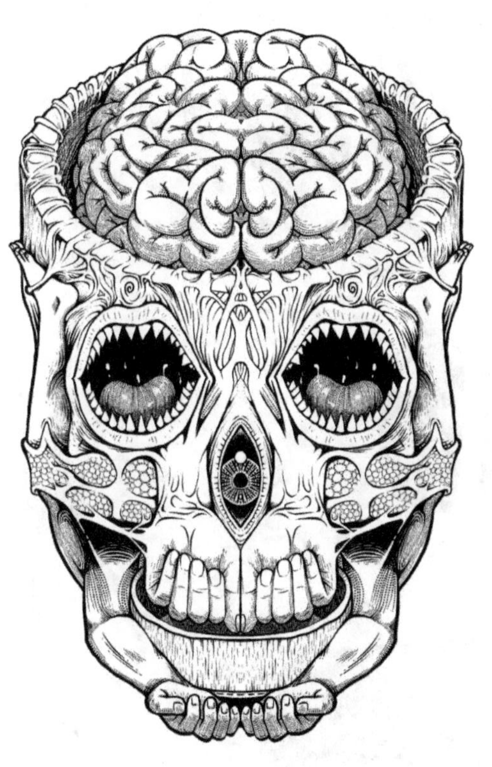

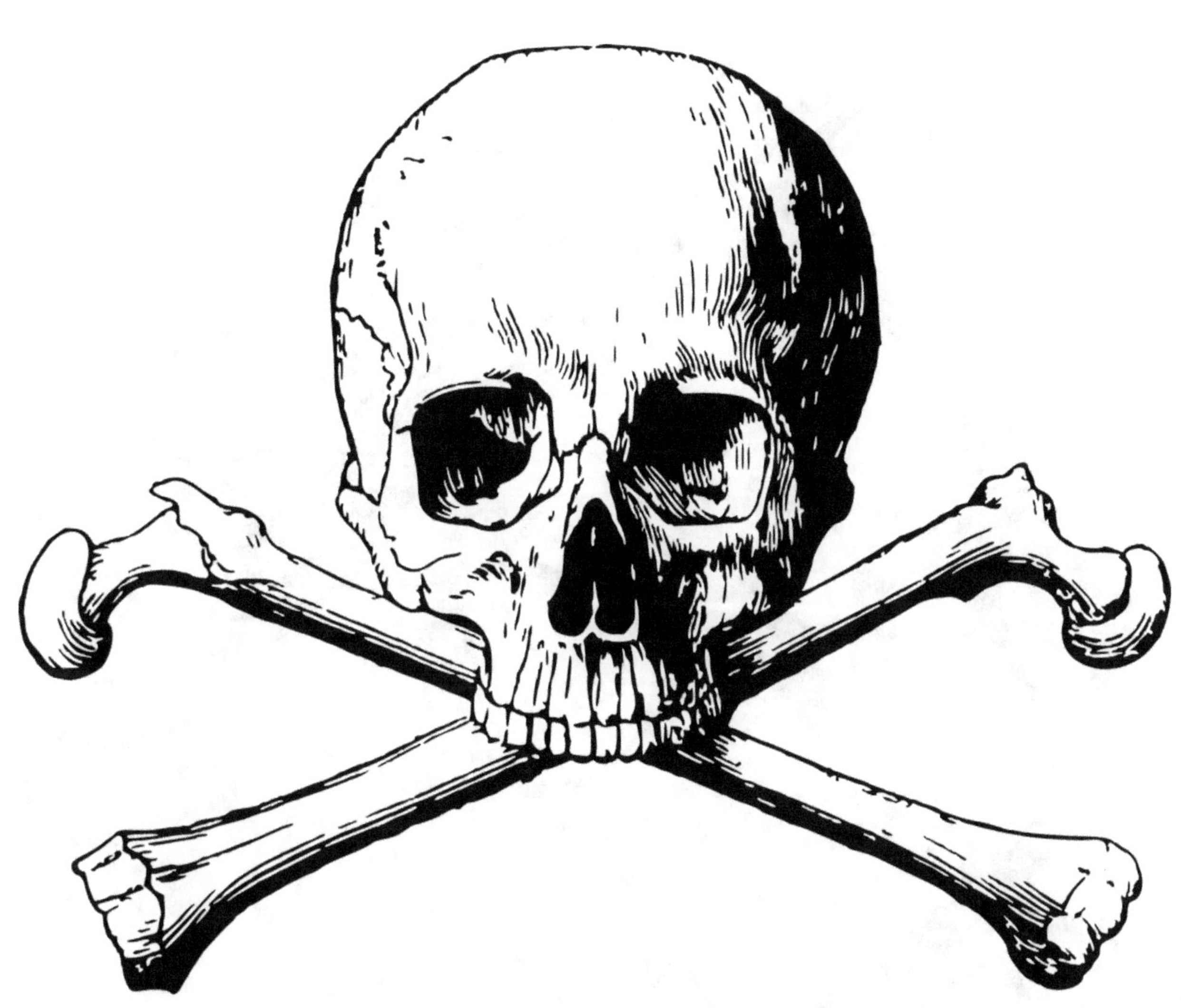

WOW THOSE WERE SCARY WELL HOPE YOU HAD FUN AND GOD BLESS

www.ingramcontent.com/pod-product-compliance
Lightning Source LLC
LaVergne TN
LVHW080039170826
845677LV00025B/1489